Cheer Up, Mouse!

Jed Henry

Houghton Mifflin Books for Children Houghton Mifflin Harcourt Boston New York 2012

Houghton Mifflin Books for Children is an imprint of Houghton Mifflin Harcourt Publishing Company.

www.hmhbooks.com

The text of this book is set in Arlt Blanca. The illustrations were created with watercolors, pastels, and colored pencils, and digitally.

Library of Congress Cataloging-in-Publication Data is on file.

ISBN 978-0-547-68107-8

Manufactured in Malaysia
TWP 10 9 8 7 6 5 4 3 2

4500398857

For Mom,
with thanks for my childhood.

And also for Kate O'Sullivan,
who loves Mouse as much as I do.

How are we going to make Mouse smile?

I know how to pick him up.

Flap and flutter, dip and dive—
Cheer up, Mouse!

Dizzy heights are for the birds.
I can wash those tears away.

Splash and paddle, wash and wade—
Cheer up, Mouse!

Looks like Mouse is sinking deeper.
I can make him jump for joy.

Leap and lope, hop and jump—
Cheer up, Mouse!

All that bouncing shook him up.
I'll put him back on solid ground.

Dig and shovel,
root and tunnel—
Cheer up, Mouse!

Low-down digging is the pits.
I'll carry Mouse above the gloom.

Skip and skitter,
climb and clamber—
Cheer up, Mouse!

Now he's stuck out on a limb,
but we can make his spirit sing.

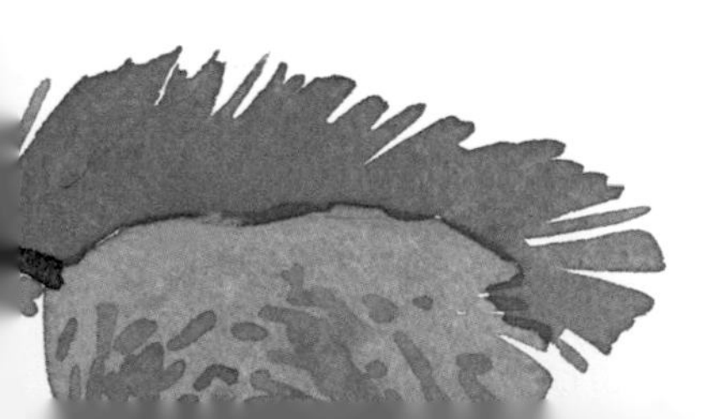

Chirp and whistle, pipe and hum—
Cheer up, Mouse!

Singing won't fill Mouse's stomach.
Hearty grub is what he needs.

Chomp and chew,
crunch and munch—
Cheer up, Mouse!

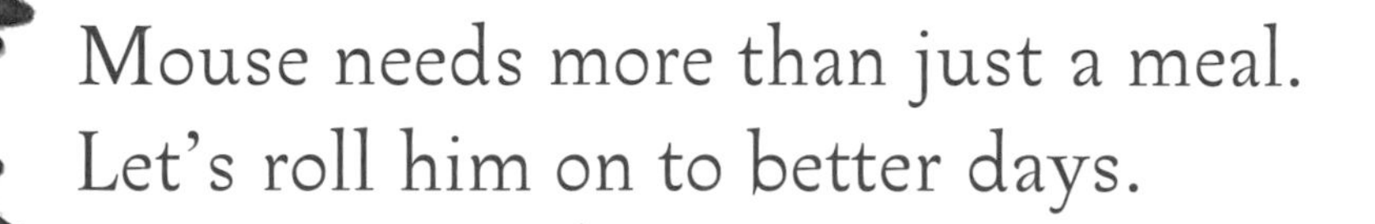

Mouse needs more than just a meal.
Let's roll him on to better days.

Tuck and tumble, flip and flop—
Cheer up, Mouse!

Hey, where's Mouse going?

Cheer up, Mouse!